TO SLEEP

James Sage

illustrated by Warwick Hutton

Margaret K. McElderry Books
NEW YORK

For My Mother

J.S.

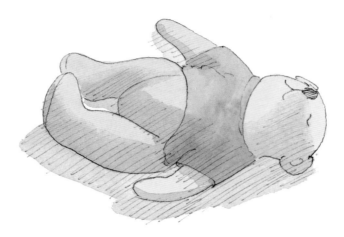

Text copyright © 1990 by James Sage
Illustrations copyright © 1990 by Warwick Hutton

Margaret K. McElderry Books
Macmillan Publishing Company
866 Third Avenue
New York, New York 10022
Collier Macmillan Canada, Inc.

First Edition
Printed in Hong Kong
10 9 8 7 6 5 4 3 2 1

Library of Congress Cataloging-in-Publication Data
Sage, James.
To sleep / James Sage; illustrated by Warwick Hutton. — 1st ed.
p.   cm.
Summary: A mother explains to her child why it's time to go to sleep.
[1. Bedtime—Fiction.   2. Sleep—Fiction.]   I. Hutton, Warwick, ill.
II. Title.
PZ7.S1304To   1990   [E]—dc20   89-36931   CIP   AC
ISBN 0-689-50497-7

It's time to sleep," said the mother.

"But I'm not tired," said the child.

"Soon you will be," said the mother.

"We have reached the end of the day."

"Where is the end, Mother?" asked the child.

"Beyond your pillow and your bed,"
she answered. "Beyond your room."
"And what is beyond the room?"

"The garden."
"And what is beyond the garden, Mother?"

"The little path that leads to town."
"And beyond the town?"

"The countryside."
"And beyond the countryside?"
"The road to the city."
"And what is beyond the city, Mother?"

"The sea."
"And beyond the sea?"

"The mountains."
"And beyond the mountains?"

"The stars."
"What lies beyond the stars, Mother?"

"Dreams."
"And where do dreams come from?"
asked the child.

"They come from your head,"
said the mother,
"on your pillow, in your bed...
where you are safe and warm."

"Good night, Mother."
"Good night, darling."

"Good night."